BRANDON DORMAN

PIRATES OF THE SEA!

Greenwillow Books
An Imprint of HarperCollinsPublishers

Adobe Illustrator was used to prepare the full-color art.

The text type is Bembo Regular.

Library of Congress Cataloging-in-Publication Data

Dorman, Brandon.

Pirates of the sea! / by Brandon Dorman.

p.   cm.

"Greenwillow Books."

Summary: Cap'n Bones and his crew face sharks, a sea serpent, and more as they follow a map toward a real treasure.

ISBN 978-0-06-204068-8 (trade bdg.)

[1. Stories in rhyme. 2. Pirates—Fiction. 3. Adventure and adventurers—Fiction. 4. Buried treasure—Fiction.] I. Title.

PZ8.3.D7345Pir 2011   [E]—dc22   2010025820

11 12 13 14 15 SCP 10 9 8 7 6 5 4 3 2 1

First Edition

 Greenwillow Books

For me three swashbucklin' mates:
Sourpatch Sam, Jolly-Cheeks Jackson, and Mighty Max.
Ye be ME treasure.

From the deck of a wreck with a pirate flag
comes a loud and lusty roar—
It's Cap'n Bones and his briny crew,
and they're sailing away from shore!

The cannons are primed and the sails unfurled on the *Dragonfish of Doom*,
And each salty dog is bellowing, "Let the plunderin' resume!"

Onboard be Twitchin' Billy, and also One-Eyed Joe,
Who's always dropping cannonballs on everybody's toes.

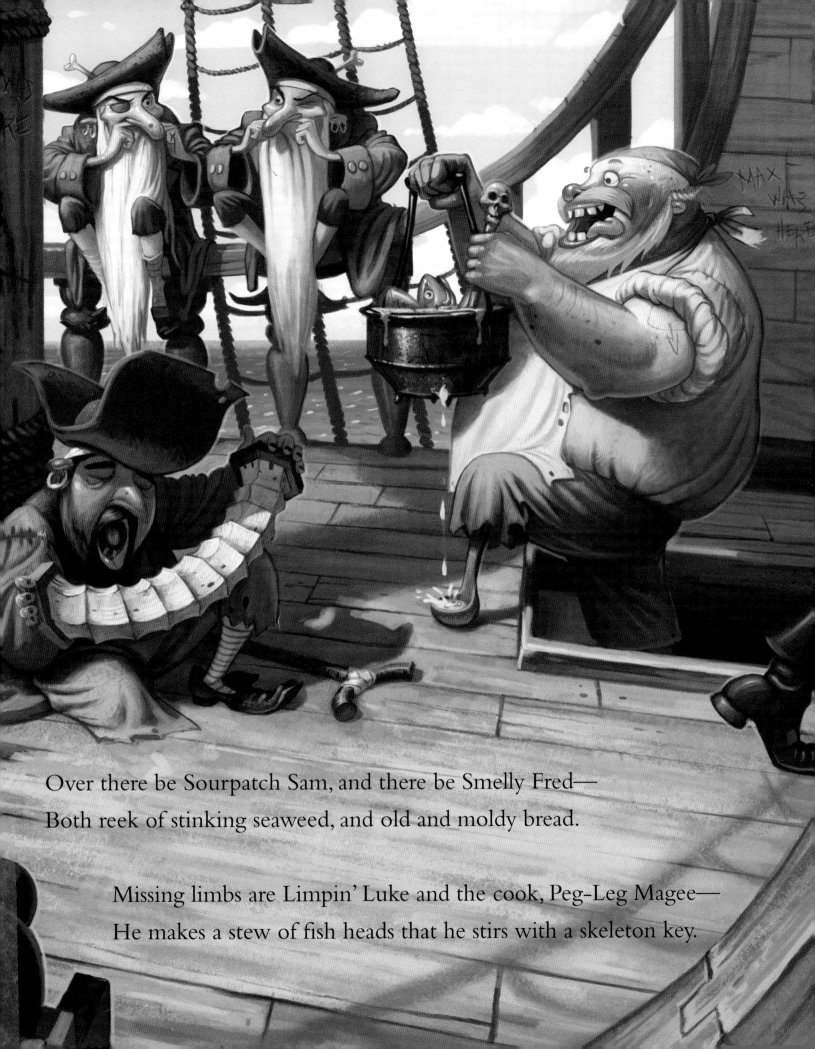

Over there be Sourpatch Sam, and there be Smelly Fred—
Both reek of stinking seaweed, and old and moldy bread.

Missing limbs are Limpin' Luke and the cook, Peg-Leg Magee—
He makes a stew of fish heads that he stirs with a skeleton key.

The sails be hoist, commands be voiced, and the winds they all be blowed!
The crew stands straight while Sea-Slug Nate yells out the pirate code:

"No cryin'
No dyin'
No brushin' yer teeth!
No stealin'
No squealin'
No eatin' Parrot Pete!
No nappin'
No scrappin'
No wimpy moans or groans!
No veggies
No wedgies
No disobeyin' Cap'n Bones!"

nd so each chum raises a thumb and plants it upon his nose.
hey cheer and cackle and sing out a chorus of pirate *Yo-ho-ho's.*

Yo-ho-ho

Yo-ho-ho

Yo-ho-ho

Yo-ho-ho

Yo-ho-ho

Yo-

"Avast, me hearties," says Cap'n Bones, as he turns to face his cre[w]
"Ye lily-livered lobsters all, you're in for horrid news."

"Our chests, they all be empty; our doubloons, they all be gone.
Spent, them was, on earrings for our old pal Long–Lobes John.

"On Terrible Tom's new teeth they went, and Jumpin' Jake's old goat,
On Seasick Sid's striped ankle socks and Clumsy Casey's coat."

"Blasted barnacles!" comes the cry. "We'll make 'em walk the plank!
Just like they did under William Kidd and that blaggard Heartless Hank."

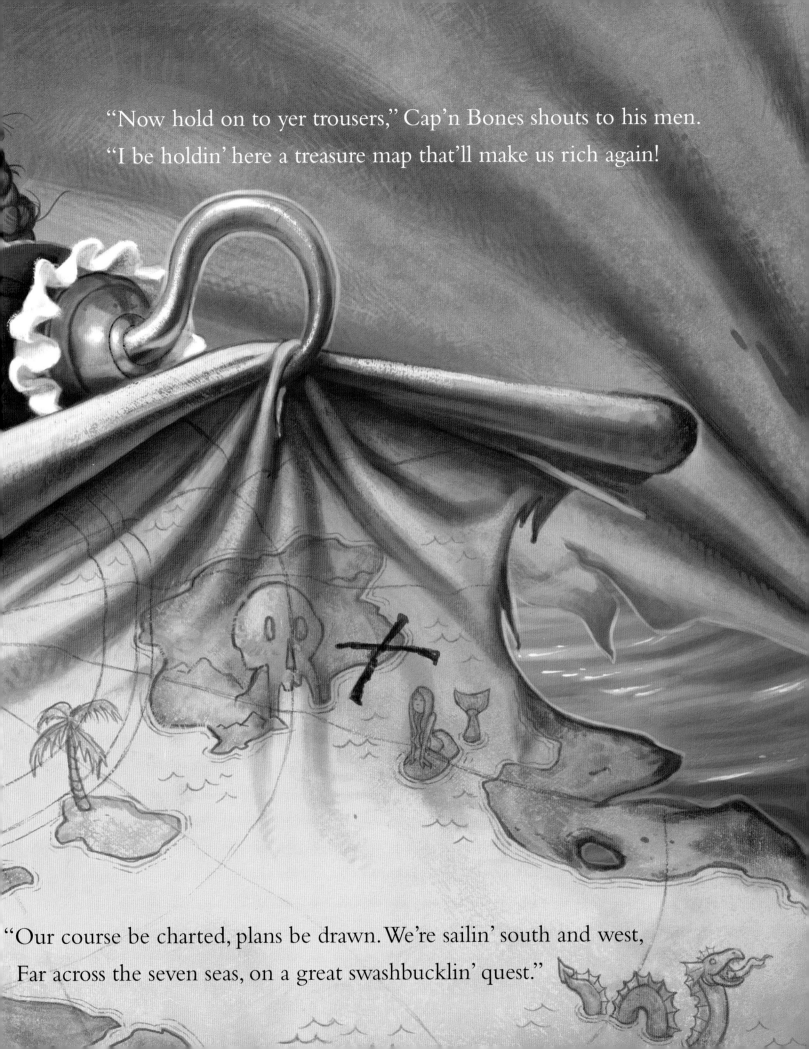

"Now hold on to yer trousers," Cap'n Bones shouts to his men.
"I be holdin' here a treasure map that'll make us rich again!

"Our course be charted, plans be drawn. We're sailin' south and west,
Far across the seven seas, on a great swashbucklin' quest."

They follow their map as the sails snap, for a day and then a night,
But then some sly and hungry sharks swim by to take a bite.

Their teeth get hold of Burpin' Bart, and they chomp him in the rear,
So Fiddlin' Flynn, he does them in, without a note of fear.

"Yo-ho!" They've fled, they've swum away! The pirates have prevailed . . .
They hardly notice they've run aground on a HUGE sea monster's tail!

The serpent prepares his toothy jaws for this pirate-packed parfait,
But Cap'n Bones spits in his eye and—"*Hooray!*"—he saves the day.

Hooray!

On morning tide, they sail inside a sandy blue lagoon,
Where mermaids swim while pirates grin and sing a lovesick tune.

Gunpowder Gus leans overboard to catch a sweetheart's kiss,
But all he gets for his puckerings are the cold lips of a fish.

Then Lookout Lee, from his crow's nest perch, shouts to raise the alarm:
"Arggh! The skies are startin' to boil—it's an evil-looking storm!"

"Batten down them hatches!" Cap'n Bones cries shrill and loud,
As lightning first, then thunder spout beneath a big black cloud.

A *flash!* A *crash!* And look, here comes a gigantic white-tipped wave,
That nearly pulls Ol' Pillagin' Pat into a watery grave.

All sails be tattered and all be torn, but when the storm's all through,
On the tippy-top of Great Skull Rock sits the ship and its soggy crew.

"Blimey! Ye swabbin' sea-squids! The treasure be down below!
Into the longboats, man the oars . . .

and row

and row

and row!"

On sizzling sand the boats now land, full of pirates ready to dig.
Out jumps each scurvy cat and dog and does a spontaneous jig.

"Dig down deep!" yells Cap'n Bones, and gives a sour last word.
He's checking his treasured treasure map, when shovel on metal is heard!

"Shiver me timbers! Be that a *chest* in that deepest darkest hole?"
"Aye, 'tis true," cries Crab-Face Chuck (along with Jellyfish Joel).

They hold their breath; they blast the lock,
And every jaw drops open in shock.

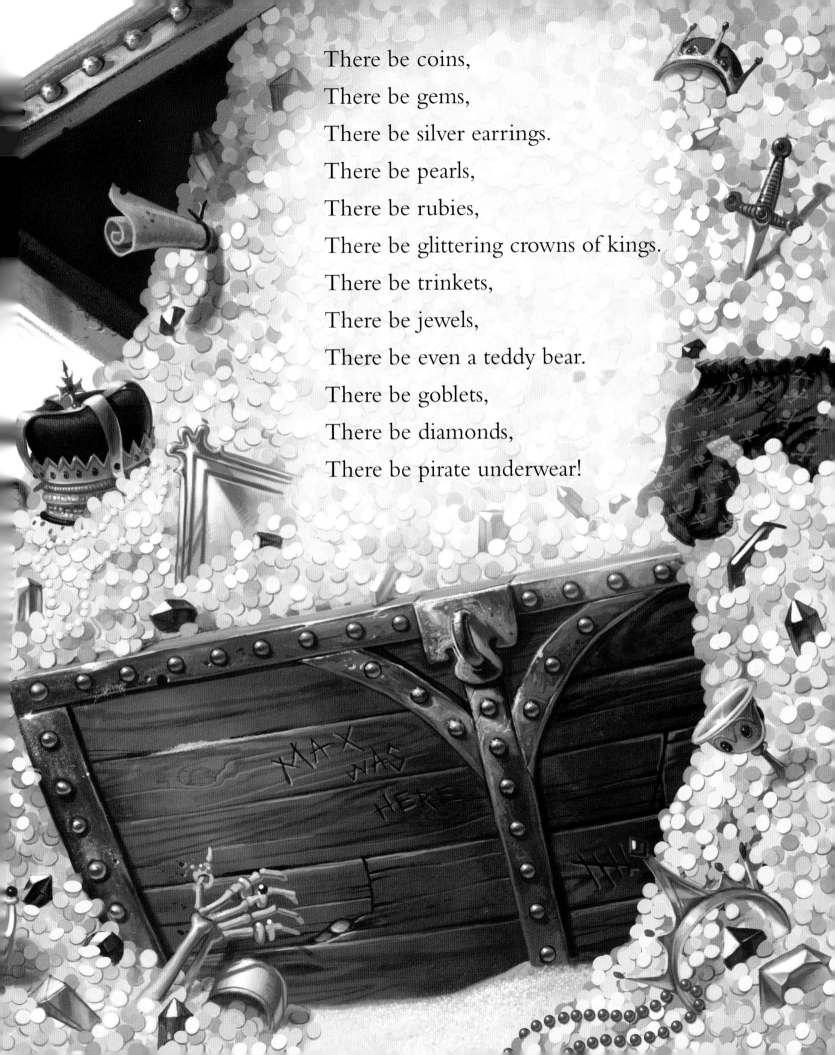

There be coins,

There be gems,

There be silver earrings.

There be pearls,

There be rubies,

There be glittering crowns of kings.

There be trinkets,

There be jewels,

There be even a teddy bear.

There be goblets,

There be diamonds,

There be pirate underwear!

Then Landlubber Jones calls Cap'n Bones, and gathers the rest of the crew.
"Let's buy lace britches—we've oodles of riches—and start our lives anew."

But back on deck on their glorious wreck, they consider what he's proposed—
Each seaweed-brain begins to strain at the thought of those stiff clean clothes.

"Never!" they shout.
"We pledge and agree."

"We're pirates!
We're *pirates*!
Pirates of the sea!"